S0-AEO-041

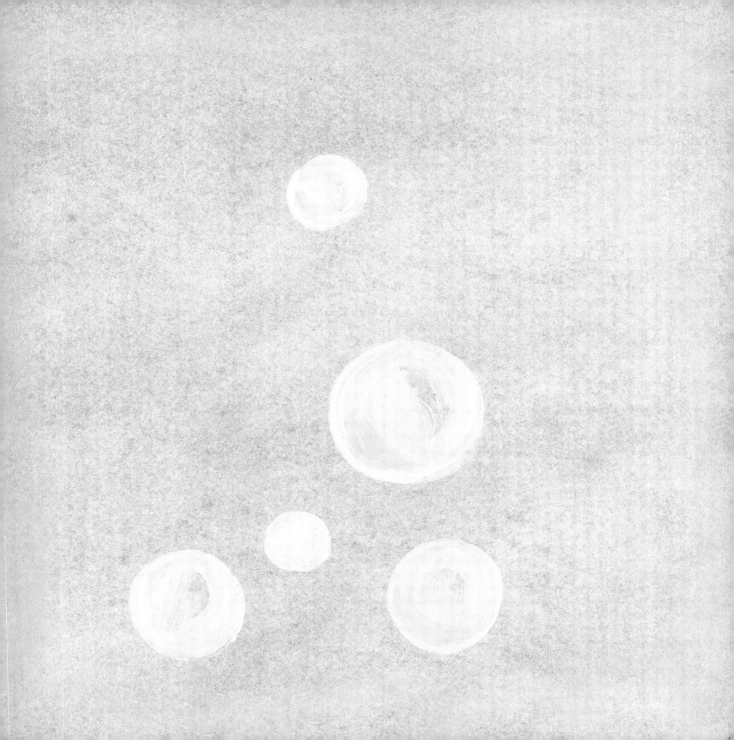

DOES AN ELEPHANT TAKE A BATH?

Fred Ehrlich, M.D.

Pictures by Emily Bolam

🍎 Blue Apple Books

Maplewood, N.J.

Text copyright © 2005 by Fred Ehrlich
Illustrations copyright © 2005 by Emily Bolam
CIP Data is available.
Published in the United States 2005 by
🍎 Blue Apple Books
515 Valley Street, Maplewood, N.J. 07040
www.blueapplebooks.com
Distributed in the U.S. by Chronicle Books

First Edition
Printed in China
ISBN: 1-59354-111-2
1 3 5 7 9 10 8 6 4 2

Who takes a bath?

Does an elephant?

Not exactly.
An elephant takes a shower
to soften its thick skin.

Does a black rhino take a bath?

No, not a tub bath.
A mud bath!

A mud bath is the rhino's way of cooling off
and soothing painful bug bites.

Does a zebra
take a bath?

Never.
But zebras often take dust baths.

The dust cools their skin and gets rid of
ticks and fleas hiding in their fur.

Does a giraffe
take a bath?

No, you will never see a giraffe take a bath.
A giraffe has a very long tongue, which it uses
to clean itself—just like you use a washcloth.

A mother giraffe uses
her tongue to clean
her baby's ears.

So do mother lions
and mother cats.

Does a beaver take a bath?

Well, sort of—if you think of a river as a bathtub.

After soaking in the water,
the beaver smoothes
its fur with its teeth.

Beavers have a special split toenail on each hind foot.
They use these double toenails like combs.

Many animals who spend lots of time in the water come out to groom themselves.

A pelican uses its beak to spread
oil on its feathers.

After a long swim, penguins help each other
preen their feathers with oil.

All animals keep themselves clean
in their own special ways.

Some lick.

Some pick.

Some soak.

Some scratch.

Some animals have helpers
to keep themselves clean.

Two prairie dogs take turns looking for insects and
picking them out of each other's fur.

Baboons clean each other's fur
just like prairie dogs do.

Only people take baths or showers to keep themselves clean.

Babies and small children cannot
keep clean all by themselves.

When bath time comes around, they need
grown-ups to help them get clean.

Like animals,
people also have helpers:

to clean their nails

to wash their hair

to trim their beards

to cut their hair

Keeping clean is an important job
for all creatures, large and small.

How do you keep clean?